D0821187

The
Godson

Leo

Tolstoy

The

Godson

Compiled by Lawrence Jordan

Fleming H. Revell
A Division of Baker Book House Co
Grand Rapids, Michigan 49516

Published by Fleming H. Revell
a division of Baker Book House Company
P.O. Box 6287, Grand Rapids, MI 49516-6287

Printed in the United States of America

Library of Congress Cataloging-in-Publication Data

Tolstoy, Leo, graf, 1828–1910.
  [Short stories. English. Selections]
  The godson / Leo Tolstoy ; compiled by Lawrence Jordan.
    p.   cm.
  Translated from Russian.
  Contents: The godson—The Devil's persistent, but God is resistant—The two old men.
    ISBN 0-8007-1792-9 (cloth)
    1. Tolstoy, Leo, graf, 1828–1910—Translations into English.
I. Jordan, Lawrence. II. Title.
PG3366.A13 J58 2001b
891.73'3—dc21   2001019916

Unless otherwise indicated, Scripture quotations are from the King James Version of the Bible.

For current information about all releases from Baker Book House, visit our web site:

http://www.bakerbooks.com

Contents

Acknowledgments

ll of the stories in this collection were translated by Nathan Haskell Dole. All unascribed footnotes are by the translator.

I remain extremely grateful to Lonnie Hull DuPont, my editor who has steadfastly stood by these stories and persistently insisted that they should be made available to as many readers as possible. Again, thank you, Lonnie.

And, again, thanks to Chinita, who constantly reminds me that loving kindness always draws out the good and that "the only thing that counts is faith, expressing itself through love."

Introduction

The inability to make a moral commitment clearly and decisively and promptly and to stick by it may be the major weakness in this nation's character, with all its other abundant, affirmative qualities. . . . One thing they lacked: the capacity to seize promptly the initiative in a right cause and to make whatever sacrifice, over however long a period necessary, to bring that decision to a successful issue. . . . To see the right and to seize it and to serve it no matter the cost is God's mandate. . . . How a soul bears itself at those crossroads of decisions determines the difference between success and failure.

Gardner C. Taylor, "A Sermon About Failure"[1]

n the three stories in this collection, Leo Tolstoy explores a question that has perplexed Christians and non-Christians for centuries: How can the

Christian life be lived victoriously? Are we able to stand up for right no matter what the cost, no matter how long the struggle? Gardner Taylor's great insight into the American national character applies aptly well to Christians in general. Christians do not always practice what they profess to believe.

Throughout history this has been one of the chief criticisms of Christians: We don't practice what we preach. Christ knew this would be one of the areas of our greatest trials and an area in which we would need strengthening: "If you love me, you will obey what I command" (John 14:15 NIV). "By this all men will know that you are my disciples, if you love one another" (John 13:35 NIV). And this to Peter, "Simon son of John, do you love me? . . . Feed my sheep" (John 21:17 NIV).

The apostle Paul spends a great deal of time admonishing believers to hold fast to their beliefs, to put into practice what they profess to believe. "You were running a good race. Who cut in on you and kept you from obeying the truth?" (Gal. 5:7 NIV).

And the Book of Hebrews reminds us that the standard for our actions rests upon the shoulders of all those who have gone before us: "Therefore, since we are surrounded by such a great cloud of witnesses, let us throw off everything that hinders and the sin that so easily entangles, and let us run with perseverance the race marked out for us" (Heb. 12:1 NIV).

To walk the Christian life, we must put our faith into action, no matter the cost. There is no victorious life for the Christian, indeed, there is no real life at all for the Christian without expressing faith through actions. Tolstoy explores this theme in the stories that follow in a simple and direct manner.

In "The Godson," written in 1886, a poor peasant can find no one in his village or the surrounding villages to be godfather to his newborn son. He meets a passerby, a stranger, who agrees to stand as godfather to his son, and the stranger assures him that the rich storekeeper's daughter in his village will gladly be the child's godmother as well. All occurs exactly as the stranger says. But after the ceremony the stranger disappears without ever revealing his name and whereabouts: "And they knew not who he was. And they did not see him from that time forth."

Later, when the godson comes of age, he goes looking for this mysterious godfather. His quest consumes the rest of his life and ultimately leads him to an understanding of the only way to destroy the evil that exists in men.

In "The Devil's Persistent, but God Is Resistant," written in 1885, a servant under the Devil's influence schemes against his good master, hoping to make the master angry enough to sin. Instead, the good master looks heavenward to find his answer.

"The Two Old Men," written in 1885, is a meditative discourse on worship, how God requires worship from us "in spirit and in truth." Two old men, one rich in worldly goods, the other not worldly rich but enormously wealthy in spiritual matters, have vowed to go together and worship God in Jerusalem. After many delays caused by the rich man's concerns, they finally start their journey. One man reaches Jerusalem, one does not. Through their different journeys, they each learn what it is that God requires from all believers.

In the years since I first became aware of these stories and began efforts to get them back in print, the one overwhelming question I have struggled with is this: Why have these stories long languished out of print, mostly unknown to the worldwide church community?

To be sure, there have been editions of Tolstoy's "gospel" stories published by publishers in the United States, notably in the 1950s, and several Christian publishers have previously published editions of the stories as well. But why have the stories not "caught on" with the body of Christ? Why no C. S. Lewis–type reception for Tolstoy's Christian works? No enshrinement into the canon of must read Christian classics?

I still have no answers to these questions, but I have an absolute assurance that bringing these stories to the attention of the reading public is essential. Scripture says, "The kingdom of heaven is like a merchant looking for fine pearls. When he found one of great value, he went away and sold everything he had and bought it" (Matt. 13:45–46 NIV). These stories are pearls of great value. When you encounter them, pass along the knowledge of their existence to others, so that many will come to know not only the Leo Tolstoy of *War and Peace* and *Anna Karenina,* but Tolstoy the Christian as well.

Lawrence Jordan
New York City

Notes

1. Gardner C. Taylor, "A Sermon About Faith," *The Words of Gardner Taylor,* vol. 1, *NBC Radio Sermons, 1959–1970,* comp. Edward L. Taylor (Valley Forge, Pa.: Judson Press, 1999), 92.

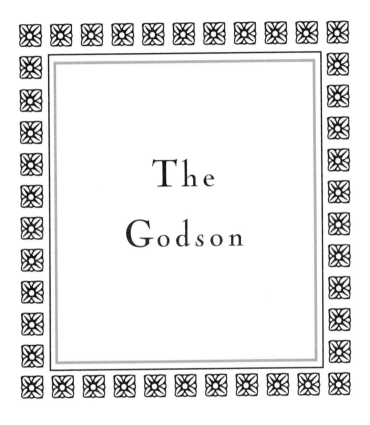

The
Godson

※ ※ ※

Ye have heard that it hath been said, An eye for an eye, and a tooth for a tooth: but I say unto you, That ye resist not evil: but whosoever shall smite thee on thy right cheek, turn to him the other also.

Matthew 5:38–39

Vengeance is mine; I will repay.

Romans 12:19

※ ※ ※

The Godson

1

A son was born to a poor muzhik. The muzhik was glad; went to invite a neighbor to be his godfather. The neighbor declined. People are not eager to stand as godparents to a poor muzhik. The poor muzhik went to another; this one also declined.

He went through all the village: no one was willing to stand as godfather. The muzhik went to the next village. And a passer-by happened to meet him as he was going. The passer-by stopped.

"Good-morning," said he, "little muzhik, whither doth God lead you?"

"The Lord," says the muzhik, "has given me a little child, as a care during infancy, as a consolation for old age, and to pray for my soul when I am dead. But, because I am poor, no one in our village will stand as godfather. I am trying to find a godfather."

And the passer-by said:

"Take me for his godfather."

The muzhik was glad, thanked the passer-by, and said:

"Whom now can I get for godmother?"

"Well, for godmother," said the passer-by, "invite the storekeeper's daughter. Go into town; on the market-place is a stone house with shops; as you go into the house, ask the merchant to let his daughter be godmother."

The muzhik had some misgivings.

"How, godfather elect," says he, "can I go to the merchant, a rich man? He will scorn me; he won't let his daughter go."

"That's not for you to worry about. Go ask him. Be ready tomorrow morning. I will come to the christening."

The poor muzhik returned home; went to the city, to the merchant's. He reined up his horse in the dvor. The merchant himself came out.

"What is needed?" he asked.

"Look here, Mr. Merchant. The Lord has given me a little child, as a care during infancy, as a consolation for old age, and to pray for my soul when I am dead. Pray, let your daughter be his godmother."

"But when is the christening?"

"Tomorrow morning."

"Well; very good. God be with you! She shall come tomorrow to the mass."

On the next day the godmother came; the godfather also came: they christened the child. As soon as they had christened the child, the godfather went off, and they knew not who he was. And they did not see him from that time forth.

2

The lad began to grow, to the delight of his parents; and he was strong and industrious, and intelligent and gentle. He reached the age of ten. His parents had him taught to read and write. What others took five years to learn, this lad learned in one year. And there was nothing left for him to learn.

Holy Week came. The lad went to his godmother, gave her the usual Easter salutation, returned home, and asked:

"Batyushka and matushka,[1] where does my godfather live? I should like to go to him, to give him Easter greetings."

And the father said to him:

"We know not, my dear little son, where thy godfather lives. We ourselves are sorry about it. We have not seen him since the day when he was at thy christening. And we have not heard of him, and we know not where he lives; we know not whether he is alive."

The son bowed low to his father, to his mother:

"Let me go, batyushka and matushka, and find my godfather. I wish to go to him and exchange Easter greetings."

The father and the mother let their son go. And the boy set forth to find his godfather.

3

The lad set forth from home, and walked along the highway. He walked half a day; a passer-by met him. The passer-by halted.

"Good-afternoon, lad," said he; "whither does God lead thee?"

And the boy replied, "I went," says he, "to my dear godmother, to give her Easter greetings. I went back home. I asked my parents where my godfather lived; I wished to exchange Easter greetings with him. My parents said, 'We know not, little son, where thy godfather lives. From the day when he was at thy christening, he has been gone from us; and we know nothing about him, and we know not whether he is alive.' And I had a desire to see my godfather, and so I am on my way to find him."

And the passer-by said:

"I am thy godfather."

The lad was delighted and exchanged Easter greetings with his godfather.

"And where," said he, "dear godfather, art thou preparing to go now? If in our direction, then come to our house; but if to thy own house, then I will go with thee."

And the godfather said:

"I have not time now to go to thy house; I have business in the villages. But I shall be at home tomorrow. Then come to me."

"But how, batyushka, shall I get to thee?"

"Well, then, go always toward the sunrise, always straight ahead. Thou wilt reach a forest; thou wilt see in the midst of the forest a clearing. Sit down in this clearing, rest, and notice what there may be there. Thou wilt come through the forest; thou wilt see a park, and in the park a palace with a golden roof. That is my house. Go up to the gates. I myself will meet thee there."

Thus said the godfather, and disappeared from his godson's eyes.

4

The lad went as his godfather had bidden him. He went and he went; he reached the forest. He walked into the clearing, and sees in the midst of the meadow a pine tree, and on the pine tree a rope fastened to a branch, and on the rope an oaken log weighing three puds.[2] And under the log was a trough with honey.

While the boy was pondering why the honey was put there, and why the log was hung, he heard a crackling in the forest, and he saw some bears coming—a she-bear in advance, behind her a yearling, and then three young cubs. The she-bear stretched out her nose, and marched straight for the trough, and the young bears after her. The she-bear thrust her snout into the honey. She called her cubs: the cubs gamboled up to her, pressed up to the trough. The log swung off a little, came back, jostled the cubs. The she-bear saw it, and pushed the log with her paw. The log swung off a little farther, again came back, struck in the midst of the cubs, one on the back, one on the head.

The cubs began to whine, and jumped away. The she-bear growled, clutched the log with both paws above her head, pushed it away from her. The log flew high. The yearling bounded up to the trough, thrust its snout into the honey, and began to munch; and the others to come up again. They had not time to get there before the log returned, struck the yearling in the head, and killed him with the blow.

The she-bear growled more fiercely than before, clutched the log, and pushed it up with all her might. The log flew higher than the branch; even the rope slackened. The she-bear went to the trough, and all the cubs behind her. The log flew, flew up; stopped, fell back. The lower it falls, the swifter it falls. It goes very swiftly; it flew back toward the she-bear. It struck her a tremendous blow on the pate. The she-bear rolled over, stretched out her legs, and breathed her last. The cubs ran away.

5

The lad was amazed, and went farther. He came to a great park, and in the park was a lofty palace with a golden roof. And at the gate stood the godfather, smiling. The godfather greeted his godson, led him through the gate, and brought him into the park. Never even in dreams had the lad dreamed of such beauty and bliss as there were in that park.

The godfather led the lad into the palace. The palace was still better. The godfather led the lad through all the apartments. Each was better than the other, each more festive than the other; and he led him to a sealed door.

"Seest thou this door?" said he. "There is no key to it, only a seal. It can be opened, but I forbid thee. Live and roam wherever thou pleasest, and as thou pleasest. Enjoy all these pleasures; only one thing is forbidden thee. Enter not this door. But, if thou shouldst enter, then remember what thou sawest in the forest."

The godfather said this, and went. The godson was left alone, and began to live. And it was so festive and joyful, that it seemed to him that he had lived there only three hours, whereas he lived there thirty years.

And after thirty years had passed, the godson came to the sealed door, and began to ponder.

"Why did my godfather forbid me to go into this chamber? Let me go and see what is there."

He gave the door a push; the seals fell off; the door opened. The godson entered, and saw an apartment, larger than the rest, and finer than the rest; and in the midst of the apartment stood a golden throne.

The godson walked, walked through the apartment, and came to the throne, mounted the steps, and sat down. He sat down, and he saw a scepter lying by the throne.

The godson took the scepter into his hands. As soon as he took the scepter into his hands, instantly all the four walls of the apartment fell away. The godson gazed around him, and saw the whole world, and all that men were doing in the world.

He looked straight ahead: he saw the sea, and ships sailing on it. He looked toward the right: he saw foreign, non-Christian nations living. He looked toward the left side: there lived Christians, but not Russians. He looked toward the fourth side: there live our Russians.

"Now," said he, "I will look and see what is doing at home—if the grain is growing well."

He looked toward his own field, and saw the sheaves standing. He began to count the sheaves [to see] whether there would be much grain; and he saw a telyega driving into the field, and a muzhik sitting in it.

The godson thought that it was his sire come by night to gather his sheaves. He looked; it was the thief, Vasili Kudriashof, coming. He went to the sheaves and began to lay hands upon them. The godson was provoked. He cried:

"Batyushka, they are stealing sheaves in the field!"

His father woke in the night.

"I dreamed," said he, "that they were stealing sheaves. I am going to see."

He mounted his horse and rode off.

He came to the field; he saw Vasili; he shouted to the muzhiks. Vasili was beaten. They took him and carried him off to jail.

The godson looked at the city where his godmother used to live. He saw that she was married to a merchant. And she was in bed, asleep; but her husband was up; he had gone to his mistress. The godson shouted to the merchant's wife:

"Get up! thy husband is engaged in bad business."

The godmother jumped out of bed, dressed herself, found where her husband was, upbraided him, beat the mistress, and refused to have anything more to do with her husband.

Once more the godson looked toward his mother, and saw that she was lying down in the izba, and a robber was sneaking in, and beginning to break open the chests.

His mother awoke, and screamed. The robber noticed it, seized an ax, brandished it over the mother, and was about to kill her.

The godson could not restrain himself but let fly the scepter at the robber, struck him straight in the temple, and killed him on the spot.

6

The instant the godson killed the robber, the walls closed again, the apartment became what it was.

The door opened, the godfather entered. The godfather came to his son, took him by the hand, drew him from the throne, and said:

"Thou hast not obeyed my command: one evil deed thou hast done—thou openedst the sealed door; a second evil deed thou hast done thou hast mounted the throne, and taken my scepter into thy hand; a third evil deed thou hast done—thou hast added much to the wickedness in the world. If thou hadst sat there an hour longer, thou wouldst have ruined half of the people."

And again the godfather led his son to the throne, and took the scepter in his hands. And again the walls were removed, and all things became visible.

And the godfather said:

"Look now at what thou hast done to thy father. Vasili has now been in jail a year; he has learned all the evil that there is; he has become perfectly desperate. Look! now he has stolen two of thy father's horses, and thou seest how he has set fire to the dvor. This is what thou hast done to thy father."

As soon as the godson saw that his father's house was on fire, his godfather shut it from him, commanded him to look in the other direction.

"Here," says he, "it has been a year since thy god-mother's husband deserted his wife; he gads about with others, all astray; and she, out of grief, has taken to drink; and his former mistress has gone wholly to the bad. This is what thou hast done to thy godmother."

The godfather also hid this, and pointed to his house. And he saw his mother: she was weeping over her sins; she repented, saying:

"Better had it been for the robber to have killed me, for then I should not have fallen into such sins."

"This is what thou hast done to thy mother."

The godfather hid this also, and pointed down. And the godson saw the robber; two guards were holding the robber before the dungeon.

And the godfather said:

"This man had taken nine lives. He ought himself to have atoned for his sins. But thou hast killed him: thou hast taken all his sins upon thyself. This is what thou hast done unto thyself. The she-bear pushed the log once, it disturbed her cubs; she pushed it a second time, it killed her yearling; but the third time that she pushed it, it killed herself. So has it been with thee. I give thee now thirty years' grace. Go out into the world, atone for the robber's sins. If thou dost not atone for them, you must go in his place."

And the godson asked:

"How shall I atone for his sins?"

And the godfather said:

"When thou hast undone as much evil as thou hast done in the world, then thou wilt have atoned for thy sins, and the sins of the robber."

And the godson asked:

"How undo the evil that is in the world?"

The godfather said:

"Go straight toward the sunrise. Thou wilt reach a field, men in it. Notice what the men are doing, and teach them what thou knowest. Then go farther, notice what thou seest: thou wilt come on the fourth day to a forest; in the forest is a cell, in the cell lives a hermit; tell him all that has taken place. He will instruct thee. When thou hast done all that the hermit commands thee, then thou wilt have atoned for thy sins, and the sins of the robber."

Thus spoke the godfather, and let the godson out of the gate.

7

The godson went on his way. As he walked he said to himself:

"How can I undo the evil that is in the world? Is evil destroyed in the world by banishing men into banishment, by putting them in prison, by executing them?

How can I go to work to destroy evil, to say nothing of taking on the sins of others?"

The godson thought and thought, but could not think it out. He went and went; he came to a field. In the field the grain had come up good and thick, and it was harvest-time. The godson saw that a little heifer had strayed into this grain, and the men had mounted their horses, and were hunting the little heifer through the grain, from one side to the other. Just as soon as the little heifer tried to escape from the grain, some one would ride up and frighten the little heifer back into the grain again. And again they would gallop after it through the grain. And on one side stood a peasant woman, weeping.

"Thy are running my little heifer," she said.

And the godson began to ask the muzhiks:

"Why do you so? All of you ride out of the grain! Let the woman herself call out the heifer."

The men obeyed. The woman went to the edge, began to call, "Co', boss, co', boss."

The little heifer pricked up her ears, listened, listened; ran to her mistress, thrust her nose under her skirt, almost knocked her off her legs. And the muzhiks were glad, and the peasant woman was glad, and the little heifer was glad.

The godson went farther, and said to himself:

"Now I see that evil is increased by evil. The more men chase evil, the more evil they make. It is impossible, of course, to destroy evil by evil. But how destroy it? I know not. It was good, the way the little heifer listened to its mistress. But suppose it hadn't listened, how would they have got it out?"

The godson pondered, could think of nothing, and so went on his way.

8

He went and went. He came to a village. He asked for a night's lodging at the last izba. The woman of the house consented. There was no one in the izba except the woman, who was washing up.

The godson went in, climbed on top of the oven, and began to watch what the woman was doing; he saw that she was scrubbing the izba; she began to rub the table, she scrubbed the table; she proceeded to wipe it with a dirty towel. She was ready to wipe off one side—but the table was not cleaned. Streaks of dirt were left on the table from the dirty towel. She was ready to wipe it on the other side; while she rubbed out some streaks, she made others. She began again to rub it from end to end. Again the same thing. She daubed it with the dirty towel. She destroyed one spot, but she made another. The godson watched and watched; and he said:

"What are you doing, little mistress?"

"Why, dost not see?" she asked. "I am cleaning up for Easter. But here, I can't clean my table; it's all dirty. I'm all spent."

"If you would rinse out your towel," said he, "then you could wipe it off."

The woman did so; she quickly cleaned off the table.

"Thank thee," says she, "for telling me how."

In the morning the godson bade goodbye to the woman of the house and started on his way. He went and he went and he came to a forest. He saw muzhiks bending hoops. The godson came up, saw the muzhiks; but the hoop would not stay bent.

The godson looked and noticed that the muzhiks' block was loose. There was no support in it. The godson looked on, and said:

"What are you doing, brothers?"

"We are bending hoops; and twice we have steamed them: we are all spent; they will not bend."

"Well, now, brothers, just fasten your block; then you will make it stay bent."

The muzhiks heeded what he said, fastened the block, and their work went in tune.

The godson spent the night with them and then went on his way. All day and all night he walked; just before dawn he met some drovers. He lay down near them, and he noticed the drovers had halted their cattle, and were struggling with a fire. They had taken dry twigs and lighted them, but they did not allow them to get well started, but piled the fire with wet brushwood. The brushwood began to hiss; the fire went out. The drovers took more dry stuff, kindled it, again piled on the wet brushwood. Again it went out. They struggled long, but could not kindle the fire.

And the godson said:

"Don't be in such haste to put on the brushwood, but first start a nice little fire. When it burns up briskly, then pile on."

Thus the drovers did. They started a powerful fire, and laid on the brushwood. The brushwood caught, the pile burned. The godson stayed a little while with them, and went farther, and he pondered and pondered, but could not tell for what purpose he had seen these three things.

9

The godson went and went. A day went by. He came to a forest; in the forest was a cell. The godson went to the cell and knocked. A voice from the cell asked:

"Who is there?"

"A great sinner; I come to atone for the sins of another."

The hermit came forth, and asked:

"What are these sins that thou bearest for another?"

The godson told him all—about his godfather, and about the she-bear and her cubs, and about the throne in the sealed apartment, and about his godfather's prohibition; and how he had seen the muzhiks in the field, how they trampled down all the grain, and how the little heifer came of her own accord to her mistress.

"I understood," says he, "that it is impossible to destroy evil by evil; but I cannot understand how to destroy it. Teach me."

And the hermit said:

"But tell me what more thou hast seen on thy way."

The godson told him about the peasant woman—how she scrubbed; and about the muzhiks—how they made hoops; and about the herdsmen—how they lighted the fire.

The hermit listened, returned to his cell, brought out a dull hatchet.

"Come with me," says he.

The hermit went to a clearing away from the cell, and pointed to a tree.

"Cut it down," said he.

The godson cut it down; the tree fell.

"Now cut it into three lengths."

The godson cut it into three lengths. The hermit returned to the cell again and brought some fire.

"Now," said he, "burn these three logs."

The godson made a fire, burned the three logs. There remained three firebrands.

"Half bury them in the earth. This way."

The godson buried them.

"Thou seest the river at the foot of the mountain? Bring hither water in thy mouth, water them. Water this firebrand just as thou didst teach the baba; water this one as thou didst instruct the hoop-maker; and water this one as thou didst instruct the herdsmen. When all three shall have sprouted, and three apple trees sprung from the firebrands, then wilt thou know how evil is destroyed in men; then thou shalt atone for thy sins."

The hermit said this, and returned to his cell.

The godson pondered and pondered; but he could not comprehend the meaning of what the hermit had said. But he decided to do what he had commanded him.

10

The godson went to the river, "took prisoner" a mouthful of water, poured it on the firebrand. He went again and again. He also watered the other two. The godson grew weary and wanted something to eat. He went to the hermit's cell to ask for food. He opened the door, and the hermit was lying dead on a bench. The godson looked round and found some biscuits, and ate them. He found also a spade, and began to dig a grave for the hermit. At night he brought water, watered the brands, and by day he dug the grave. As soon as he had dug the grave, he was anxious to bury the hermit; people came from the village, bringing food for the hermit.

The people learned how the hermit had died, and had ordained the godson to take his place. The people helped bury the hermit, they left bread for the godson, they promised to bring more, and departed.

And the godson remained to live in the hermit's place, and the godson lived there, subsisting on what people brought him, and he fulfilled what was told him—bringing water in his mouth from the river, and watering the brands.

Thus lived the godson for a year, and many people began to come to him. The fame of him went forth, that there was living in the forest a holy man, that he was working out his salvation by bringing water in his mouth from the river at the foot of the mountain, that he was watering the burned stumps. Many people began to come to him. And rich merchants began to come, bringing him gifts. The godson took nothing for himself, save what was necessary; but whatever was given him, he distributed among other poor people.

And thus the godson continued to live: half of the day he brought water in his mouth and watered the brands; and the other half he rested, and received the people.

And the godson began to think that this was the way he had been commanded to live, and that thus he would destroy sin, and atone for his sins.

Thus the godson lived a second year, and he never let a single day pass without putting on water; but as yet not a single brand had sprouted.

One time as he was sitting in his cell he heard a man riding past on horseback, and singing songs. The godson went out to see what kind of a man it was. He saw a strong young man. His clothes were good, and his horse and the saddle on which he sat were rich.

The godson stopped him, and asked who he was, and where he was going.

The man halted.

"I am a robber," said he. "I ride along the highways, I kill men; the more men I kill, the gayer songs I sing."

The godson was horror-struck, and he asked himself:

"How destroy the evil in this man? It is good for me to speak to those who come to me, for they are repentant. But this man boasts of his wickedness."

The godson said nothing, but as he started to go off, he thought:

"Now, how to act? If this cutthroat gets into the habit of riding by this way, he will frighten everybody; people will cease coming to me. And there will be no advantage to them—yes, and then how shall I live?"

And the godson stopped. And he spoke to the high-wayman.

"People come to me here," said he, "not to boast of their wickedness, but to repent, and put their sins away through prayer. Repent thou also, if thou fearest God; but if thou dost not desire to repent, then get thee hence, and never return, trouble me not, and frighten not the people from coming to me. And if thou dost not obey, God will punish thee."

The cutthroat jeered:

"I am not afraid of God," said he, "nor will I obey you. You are not my master. You get your living by your piety," said he, "and I get my living by robbery. We must all get a living. Teach the peasant women that come to thee, but read me no lecture. And as for what you say about God, tomorrow I will kill two men more than usual. And I would kill you today, but I do not wish to soil my hands. But henceforth don't come into my way."

This threat the cutthroat uttered and rode off. But he came by no more, and the godson lived in his former style comfortably for eight years.

11

One time—it was at night—the godson went out to water his brands; he returned to his cell to rest, and he sat looking up and down the road, if any people should soon be coming. And on that day not a soul came. The godson sat alone by his door until evening; and it seemed lonely, and he began to think about his life. He remembered how the cutthroat had reproached him for getting his living by his piety, and the godson reviewed his life.

"I am not living," he said to himself, "as the hermit commanded me to live. The hermit imposed a penance on me, and I am getting from it bread and reputation among the people; and so led away have I been by it, that I am lonely when people do not come to me. And when the people come, then my only joy consists in the fact that they praise my holiness. It is not right to live so. I have been seduced by my popularity among the people. I have not atoned for my former sins, but I have incurred fresh ones. I will go into the forest, to another place, so that the people may not come to me. I will live alone, so as to atone for my former sins, and not incur new ones."

Thus reasoned the godson; and he took a little bag of biscuits and his spade, and went away from the cell into a ravine, so as to dig for himself a hut in a gloomy place, to hide from the people.

The godson was walking along with his little bag and his spade when the cutthroat overtook him. The godson was frightened, tried to run, but the cutthroat caught up with him.

"Where are you going?" said he.

The godson told him that he wanted to go away from people, to a place where no one would find him.

The cutthroat marveled.

"How will you live now, when people no longer will come to you?"

The godson had not thought of this before; but when the cutthroat asked him, he began to think about his sustenance.

"On what God will give," said he.

The highwayman said nothing, but rode on.

"Why was it," said the godson to himself, "that I said nothing to him about his life? Perhaps now he is repentant. Today he seemed more subdued, and did not threaten to kill me."

And the godson shouted to the cutthroat:

"But still it is needful for thee to repent. Thou wilt not escape from God."

The cutthroat wheeled his horse around, and, drawing a knife from his belt, shook it at the godson. The godson was frightened; he ran into the forest.

The cutthroat did not attempt to follow him, but only shouted:

"Twice I have let you off; fall not in my hands a third time, else I will kill you!"

He said this, and rode off.

The godson went at eventide to water his brands; behold! one had put forth sprouts, an apple tree was growing from it.

12

The godson hid from the people, and began to live alone. His biscuits were used up.

"Well," he said to himself, "now I will seek for roots."

But, as he began his search, he saw, hanging on a bough, a little bag of biscuits. The godson took it, and began to eat.

As soon as his biscuits were gone, again another little bag came, on the same branch. And thus the godson lived. He had only one grievance: he was afraid of the cutthroat. As soon as he heard the cutthroat, he would hide himself; he would think:

"He will kill me, and I shall not have time to atone for my sins."

Thus he lived for ten years more. One apple tree grew, and thus there remained two firebrands as firebrands.

Once the godson arose betimes and proceeded to fulfill his task; he soaked the earth around the firebrands, but he became weary, and sat down to rest.

He sat down, and while he was resting he said to himself:

"I have done wrong because I have been afraid of death. If it please God, I may thus atone even by death for my sins."

Even while these thoughts were passing through his mind, suddenly he heard the cutthroat coming; he was cursing.

The godson listened, and he said:

"Without God, no evil and no good can come to me from any one."

And he went out to meet the cutthroat. He saw that the cutthroat was not riding alone, but had a man behind him on the saddle. And the man's hands and mouth were tied up. The man was silent, but the cutthroat was railing at him.

The godson went out to the cutthroat, and stood in front of the horse.

"Where," said he, "art thou taking this man?"

"I am taking him into the forest. This is a merchant's son. He will not tell where his father's money is hidden. I am going to thrash him until he will tell."

And the cutthroat started to ride on. But the godson would not allow it; he seized the horse by the bridle.

"Let this man go," said he.

The cutthroat was wroth with the godson and threatened him.

"Do you desire this?" he exclaimed. "I promise you I will kill you. Out of the way!"

The godson was not intimidated.

"I will not get out of thy way," said he. "I fear thee not. I fear God only. And God bids me not let thee go. Unloose the man."

The cutthroat scowled, drew out his knife, cut the cords, let the merchant's son go free.

"Off with you," says he, "both of you! and don't cross my path a second time."

The merchant's son jumped down and made off, and the cutthroat started to ride on, but the godson still detained him. He began to urge him to reform his evil life. The cutthroat stood still, heard every word; but he made no reply, and rode off.

The next morning the godson went to water his firebrands. Behold! the second one had sprouted—another apple tree was growing.

13

Ten years more passed.

One time the godson was sitting down, he had no desires and he had no fear, and his heart was glad within him. And he said to himself:

"What blessings men receive from God! But they torment themselves in vain. They ought to live and enjoy their lives."

And he remembered all the wickedness of men—how they torment themselves. And he felt sorry for them.

"Here I am," he said to himself, "living idly. I must go out and tell people what I know."

Even while he was pondering, he heard the cutthroat coming. He was about to let him pass; for he thought:

"Whatever I say to him, he will not accept."

This was his first thought; but then he reconsidered it, and went out on the road. The cutthroat was riding by in moody silence; his eyes were on the ground.

The godson gazed at him, and he felt sorry for him; he drew near to him and seized him by the knee.

"Dear brother," said he, "have pity on thine own soul. Lo! the Spirit of God is in thee. Thou tormentest thyself, and others thou tormentest; and thou wilt be tormented still more grievously. But God loves thee so! With what bounty has He blessed thee! Ruin not thyself, brother! Change thy life."

The cutthroat frowned, and he turned away.

"Out of my way!" he exclaimed.

The godson clutched the cutthroat's knees more firmly, and burst into tears.

The cutthroat raised his eyes to the godson. He looked and he looked, and then, dismounting from his horse, he fell on his knees before the godson.

"You have conquered me, old man," he cried. "Twenty years have I struggled with you. You have won me over. I have henceforth no power over you. Do with me as it seems to you good. When you spoke to me the first time," said he, "I only did the more evil. And your words made an impression on me only when you went away from men, and I learned that you gained no advantage from men."

And the godson remembered that the peasant woman succeeded in cleaning her table only after she had rinsed out her towel. When he ceased to think about himself, his heart was purified, and he began to purify the hearts of others.

And the cutthroat said:

"But my heart was changed within me only when you ceased to fear death."

And the godson remembered that the hoop makers only succeeded in bending their hoops after they had fastened their block: when he ceased to be afraid of death, he had fastened his life in God, and a disobedient heart became obedient.

And the cutthroat said:

"But my heart melted entirely only when you pitied me and wept before me."

The godson was overjoyed; he led the cutthroat to the place where the firebrands had been.

They came to it, but out of the last firebrand also an apple tree had sprung!

And the godson remembered that the drovers' damp wood had kindled only when a great fire was built: when his own heart was well on fire, another's took fire from it.

And the godson was glad because now he had atoned for all his sins.

He told all this to the cutthroat, and died. The cutthroat buried him and began to live as the godson bade him, and thus became a teacher of men.

1886

Notes

1. Little father and mother.
2. 108.33 pounds.

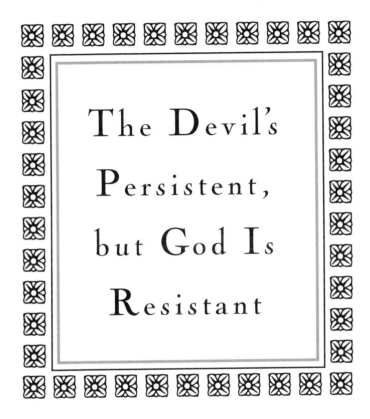

The Devil's
Persistent,
but God Is
Resistant

here lived in olden times a good master. He had plenty of everything, and many slaves served him. And the slaves used to praise their master. They said:

"There is not a better master under heaven, than ours. He not only feeds us and clothes us well, and gives us work according to our strength, but he never insults any of us, and never gets angry with us; he is not like other masters, who treat their slaves worse than cattle, and put them to death whether they are to blame or not, and never say a kind word to them. Our master wishes us well, and treats us kindly, and says kind things to us. We couldn't have a better life than ours."

Thus the slaves praised their master.

And here the Devil began to get vexed because the slaves lived in comfort and love with their master.

And the Devil got hold of one of this master's slaves named Alyeb. He got hold of him and commanded him to entice the other slaves.

And when all the slaves were taking their rest, and were praising their master, Alyeb raised his voice, and said:

"It's all nonsense your praising our master's goodness. Try to humor the Devil, and the Devil will be good. We serve our master well, we humor him in all things. As soon as he thinks of anything, we do it; we divine his thoughts. How make him be not good to us? Just stop humoring him, and do bad work for him, and he will be like all the others, and he will return evil for evil worse than the crossest of masters."

And the other slaves began to argue with Alyeb. And they argued, and laid a wager. Alyeb undertook to make their kind master angry. He undertook it on the condition that, if he did not make him angry, he should give his holiday clothes; but if he should make him angry, then they agreed to give him, each one of them, their holiday clothes; and, moreover, they agreed to protect him from their master, if he should be put in irons, or, if thrown in prison, to free him. They laid the wager, and Alyeb promised to make their master angry the next morning.

Alyeb served his master in the sheep-cote; he had charge of the costly breeding-rams.

And here in the morning the good master came with some guests to the sheep-cote, and began to show them his beloved, costly rams. The Devil's accomplice winked to his comrades:

"Look! I'll soon get the master angry."

All the slaves had gathered. They peered in at the door and through the fence; and the Devil climbed into a tree, and looked down into the dvor, to see how his accomplice would do his work.

The master came round the dvor, showed his guests his sheep and lambs, and then was going to show his best ram.

"The other rams," says he, "are good; but this one here, the one with the twisted horns, is priceless; he is more precious to me than my eyes."

The sheep and rams were jumping about the dvor to avoid the people, and the guests were unable to examine the valuable ram. This ram would scarcely come to a stop before the Devil's accomplice, as if accidentally, would scare the sheep, and again they would get mixed up.

The guests were unable to make out which was the priceless ram.

Here the master became tired. He said:

"Alyeb, my dear, just try to catch the best ram with the wrinkled horns, and hold him. Be careful."

And, as soon as the master said this, Alyeb threw himself, like a lion, amid the rams, and caught the priceless ram by the wool. He caught him by the wool, and instantly grabbed him with one hand by the left hind leg, lifted it up, and, right before the master's eyes, bent his leg, and it cracked like a dry stick. Alyeb broke the precious ram's leg below the knee. The ram bleated, and fell on his fore knees. Alyeb grabbed him by the right leg; but the left turned inside out, and hung down like a whip. The guests and all the slaves groaned, and the Devil rejoiced when he saw how cleverly Alyeb had done his job.

The master grew darker than night, frowned, hung his head, and said not a word. The guests and slaves were also silent.... They waited to see what would happen.

The master kept silent awhile; then he shook himself, as if trying to throw off something, and raised his head, and turned his eyes heavenward. Not long he gazed before the wrinkles on his brow disappeared; he smiled, and fixed his eyes on Alyeb. He looked at Alyeb, smiled again, and said:

"O Alyeb, Alyeb! Thy master told thee to make me angry. But my master is stronger than thine, and thou hast not led me into anger; but I shall make thy master angry. Thou wert afraid that I would punish thee, and hast wished to be free, Alyeb. Know, then, that thy punishment will not come from me; but as thou art anxious for thy freedom, here, in the presence of my guests, I give thee thy freedom. Go wherever it may please thee, and take thy holiday clothes."

And the kind master went back to the house with his guests. But the Devil gnashed his teeth, fell from the tree, and sank through the earth.

1885

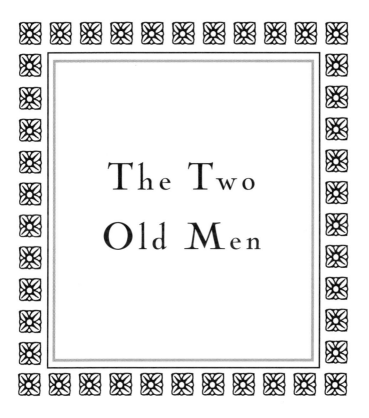

The Two
Old Men

※ ※ ※

The woman saith unto him, "Sir, I perceive that thou art a prophet.

"Our fathers worshiped in this mountain; and ye say that in Jerusalem is the place where men ought to worship."

Jesus saith unto her, "Woman, believe me, the hour cometh, when ye shall neither in this mountain, nor yet at Jerusalem, worship the Father.

"Ye worship ye know not what: we know what we worship: for salvation is of the Jews.

"But the hour cometh, and now is, when the true worshipers shall worship the Father in spirit and in truth: for the Father seeketh such to worship him."

John 4:19–23

※ ※ ※

The Two Old Men

1

wo aged men resolved to worship God in old Jerusalem. One was a rich muzhik; his name was Yefim Tarasuitch Shevelef: the other—Yeliseï Bodrof—was not a rich man.

Yefim was a sedate muzhik; he did not drink vodka, or smoke tobacco, or take snuff. All his life long he had never used a bad word, and he was a strict and upright man. He had served two terms as village elder and had come out without a deficit.

He had a large family—two sons and a married grandson—and all lived together. As for himself, he was hale, long-bearded, erect, and, though he was in his seventh decade, his beard was only beginning to grow gray.

Yeliseï was a little old man, neither rich nor poor; in former times he had gone about doing jobs in carpentry; but now, as he grew old, he began to stay at home, and took to raising bees. One of his sons had gone away to work, the other was at home. Yeliseï was a good-natured and jolly man. He used to drink vodka, and take snuff, and he liked to sing songs; but he was a peaceable man, and lived amicably with his family and his neighbors. As to his person, Yeliseï was a short, darkish little muzhik, with a curly beard; and like his name-saint, Elisha the prophet, he was entirely bald.

The old men had long ago promised and agreed to go together, but Tarasuitch had never found the leisure; his engagements had never come to an end. As soon as one was through with, another began: first the grandson got married; then they expected the younger son from the army; and then, again, he was occupied in building a new izba.

One festival day the old men met, and sat down together on the timber.

"Well," says Yeliseï, "when shall we set out, and fulfill our promise?"

Yefim knit his brow.

"We must wait awhile," says he. "This year it'll come hard for me. I am engaged in building this izba. I counted on spending about a hundred rubles; but I'm already on the third, and it isn't finished yet. You see, that'll take till summer. In the summer, if God grants, we will go without let or hindrance."

"According to my idea," says Yeliseï, "we ought not to put it off; we ought to go today. It's the very time—spring."

"It is a good time certainly; but this work is begun: how can I leave it?"

"Haven't you any one? Your son will attend to it."

"How attend to it? My eldest son is not to be trusted— he is given to drinking."

"We shall die, old friend; they'll have to live without us. Your son must learn."

"That's so; but I should like to see this job finished under my own eyes!"

"Ah! my dear man, you will never get all you want done. Only the other day, at my house, the women-folks were cleaning house, fixing up for Easter. And both are necessary, but you'd never get done. And my oldest daughter-in-law, a sensible woman, says, 'Thank the Lord,' says she, 'Easter is coming; it doesn't wait for us, else,' says she, 'however much we did we should never get it all done.'"

Tarasuitch was lost in thought.

"I have put a good deal of money," says he, "into this building; and we can't go on this journey with empty hands. It won't take less than a hundred rubles."

Yeliseï laughed out:

"Don't make a mistake, old friend," says he; "you have ten times as much property as I have. And you talk about money! Only say when shall we go? I haven't anything, but I'll manage it."

Tarasuitch also smiled.

"How rich you seem!" says he; "but where will you get it?"

"Well, I shall scrape some up at home—that'll be something; and for the rest—I'll let my neighbor have ten of my hives. He has been after them for a long time."

"This is going to be a good swarming-year; you'll regret it."

"Regret it? No, old friend. I never regretted anything in my life except my sins. There is nothing more precious than the soul!"

"That's so. But it's not pleasant when things aren't right at home."

"But how will it be with us if our souls are not right? Then it will be worse. But we have made a vow—let us go! I beg of you, let us go!"

2

And Yeliseï persuaded his friend. Yefim thought about it, and thought about it; and in the morning he came to Yeliseï.

"Well, then, let us go," says he. "You are right. In death and in life, God rules. Since we are alive, and have strength, we must go."

At the end of a week the old men had made their preparations.

Tarasuitch had money in the house. He took one hundred rubles for his journey; two hundred he left for the old woman.

Yeliseï also was ready. He sold his neighbor the ten beehives. And the bees that would swarm from the ten hives, also, he sold to the neighbor. He received, all told, seventy rubles. The other thirty rubles he swept up as best he could. The old woman gave him all that she had saved up against her funeral; the daughter-in-law gave what she had.

Yefim Tarasuitch intrusted all his affairs to his oldest son—he told him what meadows to rent, and where to put manure, and how to finish and roof in the izba. He thought about everything, he ordered how everything should be done.

But Yeliseï only directed his old woman to hive the young swarms of bees that he had sold, and give them to his neighbor without any trickery; but about household affairs, he did not have anything to say:

"If anything comes up, light will be given what to do and how to do it. You people at home do as you think best."

The old men were now ready. The wives baked a lot of flat-cakes, sewed some bags, cut new leg-wrappers; they put on new boots, took some extra bast-shoes, and set forth. The folks kept them company to the common pasture, bade them goodbye, and the old men set out on their journey.

Yeliseï set out in good spirits, and, as soon as he left the village, he forgot all about his cares. His only thoughts were how to please his companion on the way, how not to say a single churlish word to any one, and how to go in peace and love to the Places and return home. As he walked along the road, all the time he either whispered a prayer, or called to memory some saint's life which he knew. And if he met any one on the road, or came to any halting-place, he made himself as useful and as agreeable as possible to every one, and even said a word in God's service. He went on his way rejoicing. One thing Yeliseï could not do. He intended to give up snuff-taking, and he left his snuffbox; but it was melancholy. A man on the road gave him some. And now and again he would drop behind his companion, so as not to lead him into temptation, and take a pinch of snuff.

Yefim Tarasuitch also got along well—sturdily; he fell into no sin and he said nothing churlish, but he was not easy in his mind. He could not get his household affairs out of his mind. He kept thinking of what was doing at home. Had he forgotten to give his son some commands? And was his son doing as he was told? If he saw any one by the road planting potatoes, or spreading manure, he would think, "Is my son doing what I told him?" He was almost ready to turn back and show him how, and even do it himself.

3

Five weeks the old men had been journeying; their home-made lapti were worn out, and they had been obliged to buy new ones; and they came to the land of the Top-Knots.

From the time that they left home, they had paid for lodging and meals; but now that they had come among the Top-Knots, the people began to vie with each other in giving them invitations. They gave them shelter, and they fed them, and they would not take money from them, but even put bread, and sometimes flat-cakes, into their bags for the journey. Thus bravely the old men journeyed seven hundred versts. They passed through still another government, and came to a famine-stricken place.

They received them kindly and took them in, and would not take pay for lodgings; but they could no longer feed them. And they did not always let them have bread; and, again, it was not always to be obtained at all for love or money. The year before, so the people said, nothing had grown. Those who were rich had been ruined, and forced to sell out; those who lived in medium circumstances had come down to nothing; but the poor had either gone away altogether, or had come upon the Mir, or had almost perished in their homes. All winter they had been living on husks and pigweed.

One time the old men put up at a little place; they bought fifteen pounds of bread; and, having spent the night, they started off betimes, so as to get as far as possible before the heat of the day. They went ten versts, and reached a little river; they sat down, filled their cups with water, moistened the little loaves, ate their luncheon, and changed their shoes. They sat some time resting. Yeliseï got out his little snuff-horn. Yefim Tarasuitch shook his head at him.

"Why," says he, "don't you throw away that nasty stuff?"

Yeliseï wrung his hands.

"The sin is too strong for me," said he; "what can I do?"

They got up, and went on their way. They went half a score of versts farther. They came to a great village; they went right through it. And already it had grown hot. Yeliseï was dead with fatigue; he wanted to rest, and have a drink, but Tarasuitch would not halt. Tarasuitch was the stronger in walking, and it was rather hard for Yeliseï to keep up with him.

"I'd like a drink," says he.

"All right. Get a drink. I don't want any."

Yeliseï stopped.

"Don't wait," says he; "I'm only going to run in for a minute here at this hut, and get a drink. I'll overtake you in a jiffy."

"All right."

And Yefim Tarasuitch proceeded on his way alone, and Yeliseï turned back to the hut.

Yeliseï went up to the hut. The hut was small, and plastered with mud; below it was black; above, white. The clay was peeling off; long, apparently, since it had been mended; and the roof in one place was broken through. The way to the hut led through a dvor or courtyard. Yeliseï went into the dvor and saw lying on the earth embankment a thin, beardless man, in shirt and drawers—in Little Russian fashion. The man evidently had laid himself down when it was cool, but now the sun was beating straight down upon him. And he lay there, and was not asleep. Yeliseï spoke to him and asked him for a drink. The man made no reply.

"Either he's sick or he's ugly," thought Yeliseï, and he went to the door. He heard a child crying in the hut. Yeliseï rapped with the ring:

"Masters."

No reply. He rapped again on the door with his staff:

"Christians!"

No one moved.

"Servants of God!"

No one answered. Yeliseï was about to proceed on his way, but he listened; some one seemed to be groaning behind the door.

"Can some misfortune have befallen these people? I must look and see."

And Yeliseï went into the hut.

4

Yeliseï turned the ring—it was not fastened. He opened the door, and passed through the little vestibule. The door into the hut stood open; at the left was an oven; straight ahead was the front-room or "corner"; in the "corner" a shrine and a table; by the table a bench; on the bench, an old woman, in a single shirt, with disheveled hair, was sitting, resting her head on the table. At her elbow an emaciated little boy, pale as wax, with a distended belly, was tugging at the old woman's sleeve, and roaring at the top of his voice, asking for something.

Yeliseï went into the hut. In the hut the air was stifling; he looked around behind the oven: on the floor a woman was lying. She was lying on her back, and did not look up; only moaned, and sometimes stretched out her leg, sometimes drew it up again. And she threw herself from side to side, and the stench arising from her showed that she had soiled herself and no one had attended to her.

The old woman raised her head, and looked at the man.

"What do you want?" says she. "What do you want? We've nothing for you."

Yeliseï understood what she said; he went up to her. "I am a servant of God," says he; "I come to get a drink."

"Hain't got any, hain't got any. Hain't got anything to get it in. Go away!"

Yeliseï began to question her.

"Tell me, isn't there any one of you well enough to take care of the woman?"

"Hain't got any one—the man outside is dying, and here we are."

The boy had ceased crying when he saw the stranger; but when the old woman spoke, he began to tug again at her sleeve: "Bread, granny, bread!" and began screaming again.

Yeliseï was going to ask more questions of the old woman, when the muzhik came stumbling into the hut; he went along by the wall, and was going to sit on the bench, but failed of it, and fell into the room at the threshold. And he did not try to get up: he tried to speak. He would speak one word—then break off, his breath failed him—then he would speak another:

"Sick," . . . said he, "and . . . starving. . . . Here . . . he . . . is . . . dying . . . starvation."

The muzhik indicated the boy with his head, and burst into tears.

Yeliseï shook off his sack from his shoulders, freed his arms, set the sack on the floor, then lifted it to the bench, and began to undo it. He undid it, took out bread, and a knife; then he cut off a slice, and offered it to the muzhik. The muzhik would not take it, but pointed to the boy and to the girl.

"Give it to them, please."

Yeliseï held it out to the boy. The boy smelt the bread, stretched himself up, seized the slice with both his little hands, and buried his nose in the slice. A little girl crept out from behind the oven, and stared at the bread. Yeliseï gave her some also. He cut off still another piece and gave it to the old woman. The old woman took it, and began to chew it.

"Would you bring some water?" she said; "their mouths are parched. I tried," says she, "yesterday, or today—I don't remember which—to get some. I fell, and couldn't get there; and the bucket is there yet, unless some one has stolen it."

Yeliseï asked where their well was. The old woman gave him the directions. Yeliseï went and found the bucket, brought water, gave the people some to drink.

The children were still eating the bread and drinking the water, and the old woman ate some too; but the muzhik refused to eat.

"It makes me sick at my stomach."

His wife, who did not notice anything at all, or come to herself, only tossed about on the boards.

Yeliseï went to the village, bought at the shop some millet, salt, flour, butter, and looked round for a hatchet.

He split up some wood—began to kindle a fire in the oven. The little girl began to help him. Yeliseï boiled some porridge and kasha, and fed the people.

5

The muzhik ate a little, and the old woman ate a little; but the little girl and the little boy licked the bowl clean, and lay down to sleep locked in each other's arms.

The muzhik and the old woman began to relate how all this had come upon them.

"We weren't rich, even before this," said they; "but when nothing grew, we had to give all we had for food last autumn. We parted with everything; then we had to go begging among our neighbors and kind people. At first they gave to us, but then they sent us away. Some would have gladly given to us, but they had nothing. Yes, and we were ashamed to beg; we got in debt to every one, both for money and flour and bread. I tried to get work," said the muzhik, "but there was no work. People everywhere were wandering about to work for something to eat. You'd work one day, and you'd go about for two hunting for work. The old woman and the little girl had to go a long way off begging. Not much was given them; no one had any bread to spare. And so we lived, hoping we should get along somehow till new crops came. But since spring they stopped giving at all, and then sickness came on.

Things were just as bad as they could be. One day we had something to eat, but the next two nothing. We began to eat herbs. Yes, perhaps it was from eating herbs, or something of the sort, that my wife got sick. My wife became sick, and I have no strength," said the muzhik. "There was no way of curing us."

"I was the only one," said the old woman, "who kept up; but without eating, I lost my strength, and got puny. And the little girl got puny, and lost heart. We sent her to the neighbors, but she wouldn't go. She crept into the corner, and wouldn't come out. Day before yesterday a neighbor came round, yes, and she saw that we were starving, and were sick; but she turned round and went off. But her own husband had left her and she hadn't anything to feed her little children with. . . . And so here we lay—waiting for death."

Yeliseï listened to their talk, and changed his mind about going to rejoin his companion that day, and he spent the night there.

In the morning Yeliseï got up, did the chores as if he were master of the house. He and the old woman kneaded the bread, and he lighted the fire in the oven. He went with the little girl to the neighbors', to get what they needed; for there was nothing to be found—nothing at all: everything had been disposed of; there was nothing for domestic purposes, and no clothing. And

Yeliseï began to lay in a supply of what was needed. Some he himself made, and some he bought. Thus Yeliseï spent one day, spent a second, spent also a third.

The little boy got better, began to climb up on the bench, to caress Yeliseï. But the little girl became perfectly gay, and helped in everything. And she kept trotting after Yeliseï: "Grand-dad, dear little grand-daddy!"

And the old woman also got up, and went to her neighbor's house. And the muzhik began to walk, supporting himself by the wall. Only the peasant's wife lay unconscious; but even she, on the third day, came to herself, and began to ask for something to eat.

"Well," thinks Yeliseï, "I didn't expect to spend so much time; now I'll be going."

6

On the fourth day, meat-eating was allowed for the first time after the fast; and Yeliseï said to himself:

"Come, now, I will feast with these people. I will buy them something for the Saints' day, and toward evening I will go."

Yeliseï went to the village again, bought milk, white flour, lard. He and the old woman boiled and baked; and in the morning Yeliseï went to mass, and when he came back, he ate meat with the people. On this day the wife also got up, and began to creep about. And the muzhik had shaved, put on a clean shirt—the old woman had washed it out and gone to the village to ask mercy of a rich muzhik. Both meadow and corn-land had been mortgaged to the rich muzhik. So he went to ask if he would not give him back the meadow and corn-land till the new crops.

The husband returned toward evening, gloomy and in tears. The rich muzhik would not have pity on him. He said:

"Bring your money."

Again Yeliseï falls into thought.

"How will he live now?" thinks he. "The men will be going out to mow; he has nothing. His hay-field is mortgaged. The rye is ripening; the men are beginning to harvest it (our good mother earth has done well for us this year), but these people won't have anything: their field had been mortgaged to the rich muzhik. If I go away, they'll be in trouble again."

And Yeliseï was much troubled by these thoughts, and did not take his departure that evening; he waited till morning. He went outdoors to sleep. He said his prayers and lay down, but he could not sleep.

"I must go—here I have been spending so much money and time—and I'm sorry for these people. You can't give to everybody, evidently. I meant to get them some water, and give them a slice of bread; but just see how it has taken me! Now—I must redeem their meadow and their field. And when I've redeemed their field, I must buy a cow for the children, and a horse to carry the muzhik's sheaves. There you are in a pretty pickle, brother Yeliseï Kuzmitch! You're anchored here, and you don't get off so easy!"

Yeliseï got up, took his kaftan from under his head, unfolded it, found his snuff-horn, took a pinch of snuff, tried to clear up his thoughts; but no, he thought and he thought, but could not think it out. He must go; but he pitied these people. And what to do, he knew not. He folded up his kaftan for a pillow, and lay down again. He lay and he lay, and the cocks were already singing when he finally fell into a doze.

Suddenly, something seemed to wake him up. He saw himself, as it were, all dressed, with his sack and his staff; and he had to go through a gate, but the gate was so nearly shut that only one person could get through at a time. And he went to the gate, and got caught on one side by his sack; he tried to detach it, and got caught on the other side by his leg-wrapper; and the leg wrapper untied. He tried to detach it, but after all it was not the wattle which detained him, but the little girl holding him, and crying, "Grand-dad, dear little grand-daddy, bread!" He looked down at his leg, and the little boy was clinging to his leg-wrapper; the old woman and the muzhik were gazing from the window.

Yeliseï woke up, and said to himself aloud, "Tomorrow," said he, "I will redeem the field and the meadow; and I will buy a horse, and flour enough to last till the new comes; and I will buy a cow for the children. For otherwise I should go across the sea to find Christ, and lose Him in my own soul. I must set these people right."

And Yeliseï slept till morning.

Yeliseï woke up early. He went to the rich muzhik; he redeemed the rye-field; he paid cash for it, and for the meadow-land. He bought a scythe—the very one that had been disposed of, and brought it back. He sent the muzhik to mow, and he himself went round among the muzhiks; at last found a horse and telyega which an innkeeper was ready to sell. He struck a bargain and bought them. He bought, also, some flour, put the sack in the telyega, and went farther to buy a cow. Yeliseï was going along; he overtook two Top-Knots. They were women; and they were gossiping as they walked. And Yeliseï heard the women talking in their own speech, and he made out that they were talking about him.

"Heavens! at first they didn't know what to make of him; their idea was, he was a mere man. As he came by, it seems, he stopped to get a drink, and then he stayed. Whatever they needed, he bought. I myself saw him this very day buy of the tavern-keeper a nag and cart. Didn't know there were such folks in the world. Must go and see him!"

Yeliseï heard this, understood that they were praising him, and did not go to buy the cow. He returned to the tavern, and paid the money for the horse. He harnessed up, and drove with the wheat back to the hut. He drove up to the gate, reined in, and dismounted from the telyega. The household saw the horse; they wondered. And it occurred to them that he had bought the horse for them, but they dared not say so. The husband came out to open the gate.

"Where," says he, "did you get the nag, grandpa?"

"I bought it," says he. "I got it cheap. Mow a little grass, please, for the stall, for her to lie on over night. Yes, and fetch in the bag."

The husband unharnessed the horse, fetched the bag into the house; then he mowed a lot of grass and spread it in the stall. They went to bed. Yeliseï lay down out-of-doors, and there he had brought out his sack the evening before. All the folks were asleep. Yeliseï got up, shouldered his sack, fastened his leg-wrappers, put on his kaftan, and started on his way after Yefim.

7

Yeliseï had gone five versts and it began to grow light. He sat down under a tree, opened his sack, and began to reckon. He counted his money: there were left only seventeen rubles, twenty kopeks.

"Well," said he to himself, "with this I shan't get across the sea. And to beg in Christ's name—that might be a great sin. Friend Yefim will go alone; he'll set a candle for me. But the vow will remain on me till death. Thank the Lord, the Master is kind; He will have patience."

Yeliseï got up, lifted his sack up on his shoulders, and went back. Only, he went out of his way round the village, so that the people of it might not see him. And Yeliseï reached home quickly. When he started, it seemed hard to him, beyond his strength, to keep up with Yefim; but, going back, God gave him such strength that he walked along and did not know fatigue. He walked along gaily, swinging his staff, and made his seventy versts a day.

Yeliseï reached home. Already the fields had been harvested. The folks were delighted to see their old man; they began to ask questions—how, and what, and why he had left his companion, why he did not go on, but came home. Yeliseï did not care to tell them about it.

"God did not permit me," says he. "I spent my money on the road, and fell behind my companion. And so I did not get there. Forgive me for Christ's sake."

And he handed the old woman what money he had left. Yeliseï inquired about the domestic affairs: it was all right; everything had been done properly; there was nothing left undone in the farm-work, and all were living in peace and harmony.

On this very same day, Yefim's people heard that Yeliseï had returned; they came round to ask after their old man, and Yeliseï told them the same thing.

"Your old man," says he, "went on sturdily; we parted," says he, "three days before Peter's Day; I intended to catch up with him, but then so many things happened: I spent my money, and, as I couldn't go on with what I had, I came back."

The people wondered how such a sensible man could have done so foolishly—start out, and not go on, and only waste his money. They wondered and forgot. And Yeliseï thought no more about it. He began to do the chores again; he helped his son chip wood against the winter; he threshed the corn with the women; he rethatched the shed, arranged about the bees, and gave his neighbor the ten hives with their increase. His old woman wanted to hide how many swarms had come from the hives that he had sold; but Yeliseï himself knew what hives had swarmed and what had not; and he gave his neighbor, instead of ten, seventeen swarms. Yeliseï arranged everything, sent his son off to work, and he himself settled down for the winter to make bast-shoes and chisel out beehives.

8

All that day when Yeliseï was staying in the sick folks' hut, Yefim waited for his companion. He went on a little way, and sat down. He waited and waited, and finally went to sleep; he woke up, and still sat there; no companion! He gazed with all his eyes. Already the sun had gone behind the trees—no Yeliseï.

"He can't have gone past me, or ridden by—perhaps some one gave him a lift—and not seen me while I was asleep, can he? He could not have helped seeing me. You see a long way on the steppes. If I should go back," he said to himself, "he would be getting ahead. We might miss each other; that would be still worse. I will go on; we shall meet at our lodging."

He went on to a village, asked the village policeman to send such and such an old man, if he come along, to yonder hut.

Yeliseï did not come to the lodging.

Yefim went farther; asked everybody if they had seen a bald, little old man. No one had seen him. Yefim wondered, and went on alone.

"We shall meet," he said to himself, in Odessa somewhere, or on board ship."

And he ceased to think about it.

On the way he met a strannik.[1] The strannik wore a skullcap and cassock, and had long hair; had been to the

Athos Monastery, and was going to Jerusalem for the second time. They met at the lodgings, got into conversation, and went on together.

They reached Odessa safely. They waited thrice twenty-four hours for a ship. Many pilgrims were waiting there. They were from different lands. Again Yefim made inquiries about Yeliseï; no one had seen him.

Yefim asked for a passport; it cost five rubles. He paid forty silver rubles for a return ticket; bought bread and herring for the voyage. The vessel was loaded, the pilgrims embarked; Tarasuitch also took his place with the strannik. They hoisted anchor, set sail, flew across the sea. They sailed well all day; at evening a wind sprang up, rain fell; it began to get rough, and the waves dashed over the ship. The people were thrown about, women began to scream, and the weaker among the men began to run about the vessel, trying to find a place.

Fear fell upon Yefim also, but he did not show it. Exactly where he had sat down on coming on board, near some old men from Tambof, here also he kept sitting all night and all the next day; they only clung to their sacks, and said nothing. It cleared off on the third day. On the fifth day they reached Tsargrad.[2] Some of the stranniks were put ashore; they wanted to look at the temple of Sophia-Wisdom, where now the Turks hold sway. Tarasuitch did not land, but still sat on board. Only he bought some white loaves. They stayed twenty-four hours; again they flew over the sea. They made another stop at the city of Smyrna; at another city, Alexandria; and they happily reached the city of Jaffa. At Jaffa all the pilgrims disembarked. It was seventy versts on foot to Jerusalem. Also at landing, the people were panic-stricken; the ship was high, and the people had to jump down into boats; and the boat rocked, and there was danger that one might not strike it, but might fall in alongside; and two men were drenched, but all were landed happily.

They landed and started off on foot. On the third day after landing they reached Jerusalem. They established themselves in the city at the Russian hostelry; their passports were inscribed; they ate their dinner; then Yefim and the strannik went to the Holy Places. But to the Lord's sepulcher itself there was no longer any admittance.

They went to the Patriarchal Monastery; there all the worshipers collected; the women all sat down in one place, the men also sat down in another place. They were bidden to take off their shoes, and to sit in a circle. A monk came in with a towel, and began to wash all their feet: he washed them, wiped them, and kissed them; and thus he did to all. He washed Yefim's feet, and kissed them.

They attended vespers and matins: they said their prayers, they placed candles, and presented prayers for their parents. And here also they were given something to eat, and wine was brought.

In the morning they went to the cell of Mary of Egypt, where she made her refuge. They set up candles, sang a Te Deum. Thence they went to the Monastery of Abraham. They saw the garden on Mount Moriah—the place where Abraham was going to sacrifice his son to God. Then they went to the place where Christ revealed himself to Mary Magdalene, and to the Church of James the brother of the Lord.

The strannik pointed out all these places, and always told where it was necessary to contribute money. They returned for dinner to the hostelry; and after dinner, just as they were getting ready to go to bed, the strannik began to groan, to shake his clothes, and to search. "I have been robbed," he says, "of my *portmonet,* with my money. Twenty-three rubles," said he, "there was in it— two ten-ruble notes, and three in change." The strannik mourned, mourned; nothing to be done: they lay down to sleep.

9

Yefim lay down to sleep, and temptation fell upon him.

"The strannik's money was not stolen," he said to himself; "he didn't have any. He never gave any. He told me where to give, but he himself did not give; yes, and he borrowed a ruble of me."

Thus Yefim argued, and then began to scold himself.

"Why," said he, "do I judge the man? I do wrong. I won't think about it."

As he grew sleepy, again he began to think how sharp the strannik was about money, and what an unlikely story he told about his *portmonet* having been stolen. "He hadn't any money," he said to himself. "It was a trick."

Next morning they got up, and went to early mass in the great Church of the Resurrection; to the tomb of the Lord. The strannik did not leave Yefim; he went with him everywhere.

They went to the church. A great crowd of people were collected together, of pilgrim-stranniks, Russians, and all peoples—of Greeks and Armenians, and Turks and Syrians. Yefim entered the sacred gates with the people. A monk led them. He led them past Turkish guards to the place where the Saviour was taken from the cross and anointed, and where the nine great candlesticks were burning. He pointed out everything, and told them everything. Here Yefim placed a candle. Then some monks led Yefim to the right hand up the little flight of steps to Golgotha, where the cross stood. Here Yefim said a prayer. Then they pointed out to Yefim the hole where the earth had opened down to hell; then they pointed out the place where they had fastened Christ's hands and feet to the cross; then they showed the tomb of Adam, over whose bones Christ's blood had flowed; then they came to the stone whereon Christ had sat when they put on him the crown of thorns; then to the pillar to which they bound Christ when they scourged him; then Yefim saw the stone with two hollows for Christ's feet. They were going to show them something more, but the crowd were in a hurry; they all rushed to the very grotto of the Lord's sepulcher. There the foreign mass had just ended, the orthodox mass was just beginning. Yefim went into the grotto with the throng.

He was anxious to get rid of the strannik, for continually in his thoughts he was sinning against the strannik: but the strannik would not be got rid of; in company with him he went to mass at the Lord's sepulcher. They tried to get nearer; they did not get there in time. The people were wedged so close that there was no going forward or back. Yefim stood, gazed forward, said his prayers; but it was of no use; he kept feeling whether his purse was still there. He was divided in his thoughts: one moment he imagined the strannik was deceiving him; the next he thought:

"Or, if he is not deceiving me, and he was really robbed, why, then, it might be the same with me also."

10

Thus Yefim stood, and said his prayers, and looked forward toward the chapel where the sepulcher itself is;

and on the sepulcher the thirty-six lamps were burning. Yefim stood, looked over the heads, when, what a marvel! Under the lamps themselves, where the blessed fire was burning before all, he saw a little old man standing, in a coarse kaftan, with a bald spot over his whole head, just as in the case of Yeliseï Bodrof.

"It's like Yeliseï," he thinks. "But it can't be him. He can't have got here before I did. No vessel had sailed for a week before us. He couldn't have got in ahead. And he wasn't on our vessel. I saw all the pilgrims."

While Yefim was thus reasoning, the little old man began to pray; and he bowed three times—once straight ahead, toward God, and then toward the orthodox throng on both sides. And as the little old man bent down his head to the right, then Yefim recognized him. It was Bodrof himself, with his blackish, curly beard, growing gray on the cheeks; and his eyebrows, and eyes, and nose, and all his peculiarities. It was Yeliseï Bodrof himself.

Yefim was filled with joy because his companion had come, and he wondered how Yeliseï had got there ahead of him.

"Well, well, Bodrof," he said to himself, "how did he get up there in front? He must have fallen in with somebody who put him there. Let me just meet him as we go out; I'll get rid of this strannik in his skullcap, and go with him, and perhaps he will get me a front place too."

And all the time Yefim kept his eyes on Yeliseï, so as not to miss him.

Now the mass was over; the crowd reeled, they tried to make their way, they struggled; Yefim was pushed to one side. Again the fear came on him that some one would steal his purse.

Yefim clutched his purse, and tried to break through the crowd, so as to get into an open space. He made his way into the open space; he walked and walked, he sought and sought for Yeliseï, and in the church also. And there, also, in the church he saw many people in cloisters; and some were eating, and drinking wine, and sleeping, and reading. And there was no Yeliseï anywhere. Yefim returned to the hostelry, but he did not find his companion. And that evening the strannik also did not come back. He disappeared, and did not return the ruble. Yefim was left alone.

On the next day Yefim again went to the Lord's sepulcher, with an old man from Tambof, who had come on the same ship with him. He wanted to get to the front but again he was crowded back; and he stood by a pillar, and prayed. He looked to the front: again under the lamps, at the very sepulcher of the Lord, in the foremost place, stood Yeliseï, spreading his arms like the priest at the altar; and the light shone all over his bald head.

"Well," thinks Yefim, "now I'll surely not miss him."

He tried to push through to the front. He pushed through. No Yeliseï! Apparently he had gone out.

And on the third day, again he gazed toward the Lord's sepulcher: in the same sacred spot stood Yeliseï, with the same aspect, his arms outspread, and looking up, almost as if his eyes were fixed upon him. And the bald spot on his whole head shone.

"Well," thinks Yefim, "now I'll not miss him; I'll go and stand at the door. There we shan't miss each other."

Yefim went and stood and stood. He stood there half the day; all the people went out—no Yeliseï.

Yefim spent six weeks in Jerusalem, and went everywhere; and in Bethlehem, and Bethany, and on the Jordan; and he had a seal stamped on a new shirt at the Lord's sepulcher, so that he might be buried in it; and he got some Jordan water in a vial, and some earth; and he bought some candles with the holy fire, and he had the prayer for the dead registered in the eight places; and having spent all his money, except enough to get him home, Yefim started on the home journey. He went to Jaffa, took passage in a ship, sailed to Odessa, and from there proceeded to walk home.

11

Yefim walked alone over the same road as before. As he began to near his home, again the worriment came upon him as to how his folks were getting along without him.

"In a year," thinks he, "much water leaks away. You spend a whole lifetime making a house, and it doesn't take long to go to waste."

How had his son conducted affairs in his absence? how had the spring opened up? how had the cattle weathered the winter? how had they finished the izba?

Yefim reached that place where, the year before, he had parted from Yeliseï. It was impossible to recognize the people. Where, the preceding year, there had been wretched poverty, now all were living in sufficient comfort. There had been good crops. The people had recovered and forgotten their former trouble.

One evening Yefim reached the very village where, the year before, Yeliseï had stopped. He had hardly entered the village, when a little girl in a white shirt sprang out from behind a hut:

"Grandpa! Dear grandpa! Come into our house!"

Yefim was inclined to go on, but the little girl would not let him; she seized him by the skirts, pulled him along into the hut, and laughed.

There came out on the doorsteps a woman with a little boy; he also beckoned to him: "come in, please, grandsire, *d'yedushko*—and take supper with us—you shall spend the night."

Yefim went in.

"All right," he said to himself; "I will ask about Yeliseï. I believe this is the very hut where he stopped to get a drink."

Yefim went in; the woman took his sack from him, gave him a chance to wash, and set him at the table. She put on milk, vareniki,[3] kasha-gruel—she set them all on the table. Tarasuitch thanked and praised the people for being so hospitable to pilgrims. The woman shook her head:

"We cannot help being hospitable to pilgrims. We owe our lives to a pilgrim. We lived, we had forgotten God, and God had forgotten us, so that all that we expected was death. Last summer it went so bad with us that we were all flat on our backs—we had nothing to eat—oh, how sick we were! And we should have died; but God sent us such a nice old man, just like you! He came in just at noon to get a drink; and when he saw us, he was sorry for us, yes, and he stayed on with us. And he gave us something to drink, and fed us, and put us on our legs; and he bought back our land, and he bought us a horse and cart and left them with us."

The old woman came into the hut; she took the woman's story out of her mouth.

"And we don't know at all," said she, "whether it was a man, or an angel of God. He loved us all so, and he was so sorry for us; and he went away without saying anything, and we don't know who we should pray God for. I can see it now just as it was; there I was lying expecting to die; I see a little old man come in . . . not a bit stuck up . . . rather bald . . . he asks for water. Sinner that I was, I thought, 'What is he prowling round here for?' And think what he did! As soon as he saw us, he took off his sack, and set it right down on that spot, and untied it."

And the little girl broke in.

"No," says she, "babushka; first he set his sack right in the middle of the hut, and then he put it on the bench."

And they began to discuss it, and to recall all his words and actions; both where he sat, and where he slept, and what he did, and what he said to any of them.

At nightfall came the muzhik on horseback; he, also, began to tell about Yeliseï, and how he had stayed with them.

"If he had not come to us," says he, "we should all have died in our sins. We were perishing in despair; we murmured against God and against men. But he set us on our feet; and through him we learned to know God, and we have come to believe that there are good people. Christ save him! Before, we lived like cattle; he made us human beings again."

The people fed Yefim, giving him all he wanted to drink; they settled him for the night, and they themselves lay down to sleep.

But Yefim was unable to sleep; and the thought would not leave his mind, how he had seen Yeliseï in Jerusalem three times in the foremost place.

"That's how he got there before me," he said to himself. "My labors may, or may not, be accepted; but the Lord has accepted his."

In the morning the people wished Yefim good speed; they loaded him with pirozhki for his journey, and they went to their work; and Yefim started on his way.

12

Yefim had been gone exactly a year. In the spring he returned home.

He reached home in the evening. His son was not at home; he was at the tavern. His son came home tipsy. Yefim began to question him. In all respects he saw that the young man had got into bad ways during his absence. He had spent all the money badly, he had neglected things. The father began to reprimand him. The son began to be impudent.

"You yourself might have stirred about a little," says he, "but you went wandering. Yes, and you took all the money with you besides, and then you call me to account!"

The father grew angry, and beat his son.

In the morning Yefim Tarasuitch started for the starosta's to talk with him about his son; he passed by

Yeliseï's dvor. Yeliseï's old woman was standing on the doorsteps; she greeted him.

"How's your health, neighbor?" said she; "did you have a good pilgrimage?"

Yefim Tarasuitch stopped.

"Glory to God," says he, "I have got back! I lost your old man, but I hear he is at home!"

And the old woman began to talk. She was very fond of prattling.

"He got back," says she, "good neighbor; he got back long ago. Very soon after the Assumption. And glad enough we were that God brought him. It was lonely for us without him. He isn't good for much work—his day is done; but he is the head, and we are happier. And how glad our lad was! 'Without father,' says he, 'it's like being without light in the eye.' It was lonely for us without him; we love him and we missed him so!"

"Well, is he at home now?"

"Yes, friend, he's with the bees: he's hiving the new swarms. Splendid swarms! Such a power of bees God never gave, as far as my old man remembers. God doesn't grant according to our sins, he says. Come in, neighbor; how glad he'll be to see you!"

Yefim passed through the vestibule, through the yard, to the apiary, where Yeliseï was. He went into the apiary, he looked—there was Yeliseï standing under a little birch tree, without a net, without gloves, in his gray kaftan, spreading out his arms, and looking up; and the bald spot over his whole head gleamed just as when he stood in Jerusalem at the Lord's sepulcher; and over him, just as in Jerusalem the candles burned, the sunlight played through the birch tree; and around his head the golden bees were circling, flying in and out, and they did not sting him.

Yefim stood still.

Yeliseï's old woman called to her husband.

"Our neighbor's come," says she.

Yeliseï looked around, was delighted, and came to meet his companion, calmly detaching the bees from his beard.

"How are you, comrade, how are you, my dear friend! Did you have a good journey?"

"My feet went on the pilgrimage, and I have brought you some water from the river Jordan. Come . . . you shall have it . . . but whether the Lord accepted my labors . . ."

"Well, glory to God, Christ save us!"

Yefim was silent for a moment.

"My legs took me there, but whether it was my soul that was there or another's . . ."

"That is God's affair, comrade, God's affair."

"On my way back I stopped also . . . at the hut where you left me . . ."

Yeliseï became confused; he hastened to repeat:

"It's God's affair, comrade, God's affair. What say you? Shall we go into the izba? I will bring you some honey."

And Yeliseï changed the conversation; he spoke about domestic affairs.

Yefim sighed, and did not again remind Yeliseï of the people in the hut, and the vision of him that he had seen in Jerusalem.

And he learned that in this world God bids everyone do his duty till death—in love and good deeds.

1885

Notes

1. A professional pilgrim, of the genus tramp.

2. Constantinople, the *Tsar-city*.

3. A sort of triangular doughnut, or dumpling, stuffed with cheese or curds.